Stay-at-Home Sammy
and the
Runaway Spot
Maria Nilsson Thore

Holiday House / New York

One winter morning, Sammy woke—even though she didn't want to—with ice-cold paws, a sweaty nose and a knot in her tail. Was she sick?

Stiff and sore, she dragged herself out
of bed and into the bathroom.

Something about her fur didn't feel quite right. She scratched and poked and combed; then she counted her spots. And she saw what was wrong.

One of her five hundred spots was missing.
At a time like this, only a nice cup of cocoa
could make Sammy feel better, so she shuffled
into the kitchen.

The cocoa worked. And then
she saw her missing spot!

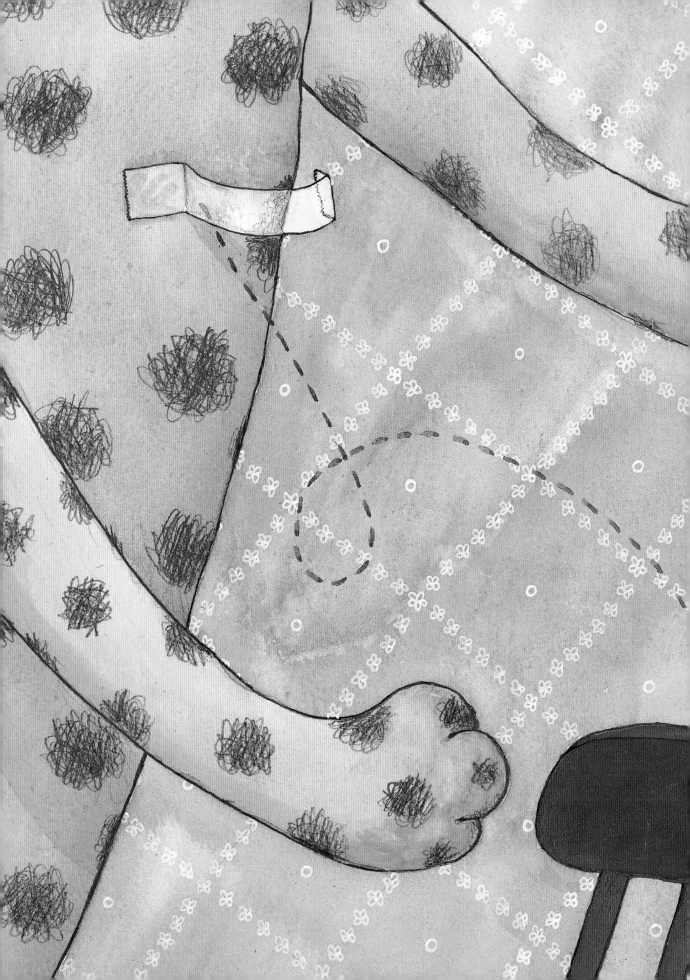

Sammy picked it up and
put it back. There!
    But the spot wouldn't stay.
Sammy chased it with tape.
That rebel spot was way too
fast.

It hopped two feet ahead of Sammy, who tipped the cup and toppled the chair. But wait! If that spot's unhappy, why pursue it?

After all, there were still four hundred ninety-nine spots that were perfectly content to live quiet lives on Sammy's fur. She decided to let it go.

Sammy opened the window, and the
spot was free.

The spot smelled of the road and of adventure. Sammy smelled of cocoa.

Though in some ways Sammy and her spot became closer than ever, their lives have never been quite the same.

To Joel, Mina & Klara

Copyright © 2011 by Maria Nilsson Thore
First published in Sweden in 2011 as PETRAS PRICK by Bonnier Carlsen, Stockholm. Gatefold,
pages 21—24 (The Eye-Opening Adventures of a Globe-Trotting Spot), first published in Sweden
in 2011 as PRICKENS RESA by Bonnier Carlsen, Stockholm.
First published in the United States of America in 2017 by Holiday House, New York, by
arrangement with Bonnier Rights.
English translations copyright © 2017 by Bonnier Rights.
All Rights Reserved
HOLIDAY HOUSE is registered in the U.S. Patent and Trademark Office.
Printed and Bound in November 2016 at Toppan Leefung, DongGuan City, China.
The artwork was created with watercolor, pencil and ink.
www.holidayhouse.com
First Edition
1 3 5 7 9 10 8 6 4 2
Library of Congress Cataloging-in-Publication Data
Names: Thore, Maria Nilsson, author.
Title: Stay-at-home Sammy and the runaway spot / Maria Nilsson Thore.
Other titles: Petras prick. English
Description: First edition. | New York : Holiday House, 2017. | "First
published in Sweden in 2011 as Petras prick by Bonnier Carlsen,
Stockholm"—Title page verso. | Summary: A spot runs away from its cheetah
and has many exciting adventures.
Identifiers: LCCN 2016004119 | ISBN 9780823436774 (hardcover)
Subjects: | CYAC: Cheetah—Fiction. | Runaways—Fiction. | Adventure and
Adventures—Fiction.
Classification: LCC PZ7.1.T477 St 2017 | DDC [E]—dc23 LC record available at https://lccn.loc.
gov/2016004119